caillou®

At Grandma and Grandpa's

Text: Joceline Sanschagrin
Illustrations: Pierre Brignaud • Coloration: Marcel Depratto

Grandma and Grandpa invited Caillou to spend the day at their house. Daddy drove him over. Caillou walked up to the front door and rang the doorbell. Ding dong! Grandma opened the door and Caillou gave her a big kiss.

Caillou ran through Grandma and Grandpa's house, poking his head into every room. He said hello to the parrot and grabbed three candies from the coffee table in the living room.

"Who wants to play cards?" asked Caillou.

Grandma, Grandpa and Caillou built a castle out of cards. When it was finished, they counted, "One, two, three!" And they blew down the castle!

Grandpa took Caillou down into his workshop.
"Will you help me paint this chair, Caillou?" Grandpa asked.
"With real paint?" asked Caillou excitedly.

"Of course. I'll show you how," replied Grandpa. Caillou and Grandpa worked together all morning.

"Guess what we're having for lunch, Caillou," said Grandma.
"Pancakes!" exclaimed Caillou.
Grandma makes the best pancakes in the world!

Caillou ate all his lunch.
"Now it's time for a nap," said Grandma.
"Can I make a tent out of blankets and sleep in it?" asked Caillou.
"Of course! What a good idea!" replied Grandpa.

After his nap, Caillou explored the bedroom.
He played with Grandma's little china dog. Then he rummaged through the closet and found a big box.

The box was full of pretty shells. Crash! Caillou dropped the box. Grandpa heard the noise and went to see what had happened.

"That's all right, Caillou. I'll help you pick everything up," said Grandpa. "Then we'll go plant flowers."

"Where are the flowers?" Caillou asked curiously.
"Inside these tiny seeds," replied Grandma.
Caillou was surprised.
"The seeds will open, get bigger and grow into flowers," Grandpa explained.
Caillou and Grandma carefully planted and watered the little seeds.

Just then, Daddy arrived to take Caillou home.
"Oh, no! Not yet!" Caillou said sadly.
"You can come back another day, Caillou," said Grandma.
"How about Saturday? We'll plant carrots!" Grandpa suggested. "Yippee!"
Caillou loved visiting his grandparents!

Text: Joceline Sanschagrin
Illustrations: Pierre Brignaud
Coloration: Marcel Depratto
Art Director: Monique Dupras

We acknowledge the financial support of the Government of Canada through the Canada Book Fund for our publishing activities.

Canadian Heritage Patrimoine canadien

We acknowledge the support of the Ministry of Culture and Communications of Quebec and SODEC for the publication and promotion of this book.

SODEC
Québec

Bibliothèque et Archives nationales du Québec and Library and Archives Canada cataloguing in publication

Sanschagrin, Joceline, 1950-
Caillou: at grandma and grandpa's
New ed.
(Big Dipper)
Translation of: Caillou: les grands-parents.
Originally issued in series: North star. c2002.
For children aged 3 and up.

ISBN 978-2-89450-656-1

1. Grandparent and child - Juvenile literature. I. Brignaud, Pierre. II. Title.
III. Title: At Grandma and Grandpa's.

HQ759.9.S2613 2008 j306.874'5 C2007-942182-2

Legal deposit: 2008

Printed in China
10 9 8 7 6 5 4 3 CHO1824 JAN2012